Getting Children Started with Books

On more than one occasion you've probably found yourself having to choose a book for a young child. As you faced an entire rack or shelf of children's books and wondered which one to select, you probably asked yourself: Which book will be appealing? Is it the appropriate reading level?

The book that you have in your hand right now is suited to children who are ages six to nine. Yearling books can be read aloud to children or they can be read independently by those children who are reading on their own.

After a child has read this book alone or with an adult, that child is ready for the suggested activities which follow. These activities follow directly from the story and provide the child with opportunities to think, to explore, and to have fun.

FUN TO READ
FUN TO DO!

After you've read
**CAM JANSEN AND THE MYSTERY OF
THE TELEVISION DOG**
here are some activities you might want to try:

1. Cam has an amazing mental camera and loves memory games. Make up a memory game to play with a friend. Try to play Concentration. Here's how: All you need is a deck of cards. Make sure your deck has pairs. Shuffle the cards, then place each card facedown. Take turns finding pairs.

2. Visit the library and find a book about how dogs are trained. What does a trainer do to teach an animal? What can an animal learn? What things can an animal never learn?

3. Make thumbprints. Press your thumb onto an ink pad and then onto a card. What does your thumbprint look like? If you have a dog, you can get its pawprint just like the trainer got Poochie's.

4. A few lines with a felt-tipped pen can turn any thumbprint into an animal, or a fruit, or a flower —or into whatever pleases you. Make a picture using thumbprints.

CAM JANSEN
and the
Mystery of the
Television Dog

DAVID A. ADLER
Illustrated by Susanna Natti

A Yearling Book

Published by
Dell Publishing
a division of
Bantam Doubleday Dell Publishing Group, Inc.
666 Fifth Avenue
New York, New York 10103

The author wishes to thank his editor,
Deborah Brodie, for her continued help,
encouragement, and friendship.

ISBN: 0-440-41196-3

Reprinted by arrangement with The Viking Press

Printed in the United States of America

January 1983

10 9 8 7 6

CW

To my nephews, Donnie, Hillel, and Jonathan
To their parents, Joseph and Arlene
And to their dog, Cloudy

Cam Jansen and the
Mystery of the Television Dog

Chapter One

It was a warm summer day. Cam Jansen, her friend Eric Shelton, and Eric's twin sisters, Donna and Diane, were waiting in a long line outside Lee's Bookstore. They were all waiting to meet Poochie, the famous television dog.

Cam pointed to a sign in the front window of the store. "It says that Poochie will be here at noon."

"That's ten more minutes," Eric said.

Cam looked through the bookstore window. Inside there was a large table. Piled

on one side of the table were books. On the
other side there was a large photograph of
Poochie and a sign that said:

Buy *The Poochie Story*
the new best-selling book by the
star of the television program *Hero Dog*.

4

Donna pulled on Eric's sleeve. "There's nothing to do. I'm tired of waiting."

Eric was holding a large shopping bag. He reached into the bag, took out a book, and said, "You could read. Is this your book or Diane's?"

"It's mine," Donna said.

Cam looked at the book. It was called *Pig Tales*. "I know this book," Cam said. "I read it three years ago when I was in the second grade. What page are you up to?"

"Nineteen."

"Page nineteen. Let me see what I can remember."

Cam closed her eyes and said, *"Click."* She always says, *"Click,"* when she wants to remember something. When people ask Cam why she says, *"Click,"* so often, Cam tells them, "It's the sound a camera makes, and my mind is a mental camera."

"There's a drawing on the top of the page," Cam said, with her eyes still closed.

"There's a pig wearing a hat and a bow tie. The pig is chasing a tractor with two roosters in it."

"What does the sign on the side of the tractor say?" Donna asked.

" 'Cluck, Cluck Farms. A nice place to live.' "

People say that Cam has a photographic memory. They mean that Cam can remember an entire scene. Her mind takes a picture of it. When Cam wants to remember something, even a detail, such as the color of someone's shirt or what is written on the side of a tractor, she just looks at the picture stored in her brain.

Cam's real name is Jennifer Jansen. But when people found out about her amazing memory, they called her "The Camera." Soon "The Camera" was shortened to just "Cam." Now the only people who call her Jennifer are her parents, her teachers, and an aunt in London who has never met Cam and never heard her say, *"Click."*

Donna turned a few pages in the book. "What about the drawing on page twenty-five?" she asked.

Cam's eyes were still closed. As she thought, she ran her fingers through her hair. Cam has what people call red hair, even though it is more orange than red.

"The pig is wearing a baseball uniform," Cam said.

"What about the stick?" Donna asked.

"She can't remember everything," Eric told his sister.

"That stick is a bat," Cam said. "And the pig is holding it in his right hand."

"You're right," Donna said to Cam. "And you're wrong," she told Eric. "Cam *can* remember everything."

Just then a long dark blue car drove up. It stopped right in front of the bookstore. The driver got out. He was wearing a dark blue uniform and cap. He walked around

the car, opened the door, and waited.

First a man dressed in white got out. Sewn on the back of his shirt were the words, "Poochie's Trainer." Then out came a dog.

"It's Poochie! It's Poochie!" the people waiting in line shouted.

Cam opened her eyes.

Poochie was a white dog with a large black spot across his back. A few smaller black spots were on his back and his right front leg.

Poochie walked slowly into the bookstore. He looked ahead as he walked, and his tail pointed up. The trainer followed him.

Cam wanted to remember Poochie. She looked straight at the dog and said, *"Click."*

Chapter Two

As Poochie walked past, a dog barked. But it wasn't Poochie barking. The man in line just ahead of Cam, Eric, and the twins was holding a white dog with black spots. The dog looked just like Poochie. The man was also holding a small open box of dog biscuits.

The man's dog barked again.

"Stop that, Cloudy. Be quiet," the man told his dog.

The man was tall, heavy, and wore eye-

glasses. And he had long red hair, just like Cam's.

Cam, Eric, and the twins looked through the bookstore window. They saw Poochie jump onto a chair and from the chair onto the large table. He sat down between the pile of books and the Poochie photograph. Poochie's trainer sat on the chair.

Mr. Lee, the bookstore owner, called out, "Say hello to Poochie. You can shake his paw. And if you buy *The Poochie Story,*

Poochie will autograph it for you."

"I'll buy a book," the first man in line said.

The man paid Mr. Lee for the book. Then Mr. Lee opened the book to the front page and gave it to Poochie to autograph.

The trainer opened an ink pad and put it on the table next to the book. Poochie pressed one of his paws onto the ink pad, and then he pressed it onto the front page of the book.

The line was moving slowly. As Cam, Eric, and the twins waited, a small boy walked out of the bookstore with his mother. The boy held up a copy of *The Poochie Story* and said, "Look what I have! Poochie signed my book!"

The boy's mother held up her hand for everyone in line to see. There was ink on it. She smiled and said, "And Poochie signed my hand."

"I guess he uses the same paw to sign the books and shake hands," Eric said.

Eric reached into his pocket. He took out some money and said, "Well, I'm buying a book for all of us to share. Poochie can use that paw to sign it."

"And I'm going to shake his paw," Donna said.

"So am I," Diane said.

"We all are," Cam told them.

Cam, Eric, and the twins were inside the bookstore now. Their turn to meet Poochie would be next. The red-haired man just ahead of them was buying a book.

The man reached into his pocket for the money. As he did, the box of dog biscuits fell onto the table. Some biscuits fell out, and the man's dog jumped after them. Poochie jumped, too.

"Get that dog and those biscuits away from Poochie!" the trainer yelled.

"Get your Poochie away from my dog's biscuits!" the other man yelled back.

While the two men were yelling, the dogs were chasing each other around the table. Books flew off the table. One almost hit Cam. The photograph and the sign fell.

"*Woof.*"

"Poochie, stop fighting!"

"*Woof, woof.*"

"Cloudy, get over here!"

The red-haired man grabbed a dog.

"Bad Cloudy. Bad Cloudy," he said as he left the bookstore with him.

"And you, Poochie," the trainer said. "You should be ashamed of yourself."

Mr. Lee put the sign and the photograph back in place. Then he picked the books off the floor and arranged them in a pile.

"Now sit, Poochie," the trainer said. But the dog didn't sit.

"Sit!" the trainer said again.

The dog barked and wagged his tail. But he didn't sit.

"There's a long line out there," Mr. Lee told the trainer. "Poochie can stand while he shakes hands and autographs books."

"This just isn't like him," the trainer said. "Poochie should sit when I tell him to."

"Whose turn is it now?" Mr. Lee called out. "Whose turn is it to shake hands with Poochie, the famous television dog?"

Chapter Three

"I'm next. I'm next," Donna told Mr. Lee.

"Then I go," Diane said.

Mr. Lee smiled. "I'll bet you two are sisters," he said.

Donna and Diane are identical twins. They were even dressed alike, so it was easy to tell that they are sisters. Only their hair was different. Diane's hair hung straight down, but Donna had braids.

Donna smiled at the dog. "Hello, Poochie," she said. "I love your show. I watch it every Tuesday night."

Then Diane and Cam shook the dog's paw, and Eric bought a copy of *The Poochie Story*. Poochie pressed his paw onto the ink pad and then onto the front of the book. Then the trainer gave the book to Eric.

As they left the store, Cam looked through *The Poochie Story*.

"It says here," Cam read, "that before Poochie became a television star, he was a real hero. A house was on fire, and he barked and barked until someone called the fire department."

Cam read as she walked. Diane held Cam's hand to keep her from walking into things. At the corner Diane stopped Cam. They all waited for the light to change.

"I'm hungry," Donna told Eric. "I want one of the sandwiches you have in the bag."

"Before you eat, you have to wash your hands," Eric told her. "You just shook Poochie's paw. Your hands must be dirty."

Donna held out her hands. She turned them over a few times and said, "No, they're not. My hands are clean."

"Let me see," Cam said. She looked at Donna's hands. Then Cam looked at her own hands and at Diane's.

"Something is strange," Cam said. "It could be that the dog we shook hands with wasn't the real Poochie."

Cam ran back to the bookstore. Eric, Donna, and Diane followed her. Cam looked through the bookstore window. Then she closed her eyes and said, *"Click."*

"What's she doing?" Diane whispered to Eric.

"Just be quiet. She's trying to remember something."

Cam opened her eyes. She looked through the window again and said, "I was right. The dog in there is *not* Poochie."

"What!"

"Look at your hands," Cam told Donna and Diane. "And look at mine. They're clean. We shook Poochie's paw. It's the same paw he used to sign the books, but no ink rubbed off."

"Maybe the ink dried," Eric said.

"That's what I thought. That's why I said, 'Click.' I looked at the picture I have of Poochie in my mind and I looked at the dog in the bookstore. They're not the same."

"How can you tell?" Eric asked. "That dog looks like Poochie to me. He's white with black spots."

"It's the spots," Cam said. "The spots on the dog in the bookstore are not in the exact same places as the spots on Poochie."

Cam pointed to the picture of Poochie on the cover of *The Poochie Story*. "Look at this and then look at the dog in the store. You tell me if they're the same."

Eric, Donna, and Diane looked at the picture of Poochie on the cover of the book. Then they looked through the bookstore window. They looked back at the book and then through the window again.

"You're right," Eric said. "Some of the spots on the dog in the store are in the wrong places."

Chapter Four

Donna ran into the bookstore. She pushed ahead of an old man waiting for Poochie to autograph his book.

"That's not Poochie! That's not Poochie!" Donna yelled as she pointed to the dog on the table.

"Of course it is," Mr. Lee said. "Now get in line like everyone else."

Cam, Eric, and Diane came into the store. Donna pointed at Cam and said, "You can ask her."

Mr. Lee turned to the dog's trainer

and said, "This is Poochie. Isn't it?"

"Of course it is. Just watch."

The trainer turned to the dog and said, "Poochie, raise your right paw."

The dog just looked at the trainer.

"RAISE YOUR RIGHT PAW!"

The dog did nothing.

"All right, Poochie, don't raise your right paw. Just show me what a sad dog looks like."

The dog barked and wagged his tail.

"He's not doing what you tell him to because he's not Poochie," Donna told the trainer.

Cam took one of the books from the table. She pointed to the photograph of Poochie on the cover and said, "Look at this and look at the dog. You'll see that they're not the same."

Mr. Lee took the book from Cam. He looked at the photograph and then at the dog.

"It's the spots. Some of the spots are in different places," Cam told him.

Mr. Lee looked at the photograph again and then at the dog.

"You're right," he said. "This is not Poochie."

"The dog I brought here was Poochie.

I'm sure of it," the trainer said. "This is only my first week on the job, but I know they wouldn't give me the wrong dog."

"It was that red-haired man with the dog biscuits," Eric said. "He must have taken the wrong dog home. This must be Cloudy."

When the people waiting in line heard that the dog on the table wasn't Poochie, they left the bookstore.

"I took time off from work to meet Poochie," one woman complained as she left.

"And I put on a suit and tie," a boy said.

The trainer sat down. He looked up at the ceiling and said, "I don't know what I'm going to do now."

"Well, I do," said Mr. Lee. "I'm calling the police."

As Mr. Lee walked toward the telephone, Cloudy jumped off the table and ran out of the bookstore.

"Get him!" Mr. Lee told Cam, Eric, and the twins.

"No, let him go. If he's not Poochie, I don't want him," the trainer said.

Cam didn't listen to the trainer. She ran

out of the bookstore and followed Cloudy.

Eric and the twins ran after Cam. They caught up with her at the corner. She was waiting for the light to change.

"Why are you following Cloudy?" Eric asked.

"They don't want this dog," Donna said. "They want Poochie."

Just then the light changed. "Just come with me and keep your eyes on that dog," Cam said as she hurried ahead.

Cloudy was almost at the next corner. Cam ran quickly down the block. The others followed her.

They followed Cloudy past a busy shopping mall and a block where some old houses were being torn down. Then the dog walked through a hole in a fence. He walked through a backyard to a block lined with small houses.

Cam, Eric, and the twins squeezed through the fence. Then they saw Cloudy run onto the front porch of one of the houses.

"I was right. I knew he'd lead us somewhere," Cam said. "Now we have to get Cloudy before he goes inside."

Chapter Five

"Here, Cloudy. Here, Cloudy," Cam called.

The dog turned and looked. But he didn't come to Cam. He lifted his paw and started to scratch on the front door.

"What's in your bag?" Cam asked Eric.

"Sandwiches and books."

"What kind?"

"Storybooks."

"No, the sandwiches. What kind of sand-wiches?"

"Meat loaf."

"Quick! Give me one."

Eric gave Cam a sandwich. She held it out and called, "Here, Cloudy. Here, Cloudy."

Cloudy turned. This time, when he smelled the meat, he ran to Cam.

Just as Cloudy reached Cam, the front door of the house opened.

"Who's there?" a man called out.

Before Cloudy could bark, Cam gave him some meat. Then Cam whispered to Eric and the twins, "Don't say anything and don't let him see us."

They were near a large, leafy bush. They hid behind it.

"Who's out there? Is that you, Cloudy?" the man asked as he stepped out onto the porch.

When Cloudy heard his name, he looked up. But then he looked back at the meat loaf and bread Cam was holding and continued to eat.

Cam pushed aside a few leaves and

looked at the man. He was bald. He was tall
and heavy and wore eyeglasses. Cam
looked straight at the man and said, *"Click."*

After the man went back into the house,

Diane whispered, "Can we talk now?"

"Yes, but quietly," Cam told her.

"Why did we run after Cloudy?" Donna asked.

"I was sure he'd lead us to his house. And I thought that when we got here, we'd find Poochie and the red-haired man who took him."

Cloudy finished eating the sandwich. He looked up at Cam. Cloudy barked and wagged his tail. Cam petted Cloudy. Then Eric took another sandwich from his bag, unwrapped it, and gave it to Cloudy.

"I don't think Poochie is here," Eric whispered. "The man we saw in the bookstore, the one who took Poochie, had red hair. The man who just came to the door was bald."

Cam closed her eyes and said, *"Click."* She thought for a short while. Then she said, "I'm looking at the picture I have in my mind of the man we saw in the bookstore. He looks like the man we just saw. Only the hair is different."

"Maybe they're twins," Donna said. "And one twin has hair and the other doesn't."

"Or maybe they just look alike. A lot of people look alike," Diane said.

As the twins were talking, Cam was petting Cloudy. Then she looked at her hand. There were black streaks on it.

Eric looked at Cam's hand and at Cloudy. Then he petted Cloudy's back, right where the big black spot was. He looked at his hand. There were streaks on it, too.

"It's these spots," Eric said. "They were put on with shoe polish or something. I'll bet Cloudy is really all white, like a cloud. These spots were probably put on so the man with the red hair could switch the two dogs."

"But where's Poochie? And why did that man take him?" Donna asked.

"I don't know," Eric said. "But I'm sure the man with the red hair knows where Poochie is."

Just then the front door opened. The bald man came out carrying a large bag of trash. Cam looked through the bush and watched as he turned over the bag. Empty boxes, newspapers, and something orange fell into the trash can.

"Did you see that?" Cam whispered. "Did you see what the man threw away? He's the same man we saw in the bookstore. Now I'm sure of it."

Chapter Six

"Did I see what?" Eric asked. "And how can you say he's the same? The man in the bookstore had hair."

"Quiet," Cam whispered as the man walked past them and back into the house. Then she told Eric, "You watch Cloudy. I'm going to get something."

As Cam walked away, Cloudy barked. "Just be quiet," Eric said as he picked Cloudy up and petted him.

Eric, Donna, Diane, and Cloudy watched Cam walk across the front lawn. They saw her lift the lid off the trash can. She held her nose and looked in. Then she reached in and took out something orange.

"What is that?" Diane asked Eric.

"It looks like fur."

Cam gently put the lid back on the trash can. As Cam walked toward the side of the house, Donna said, "It's hair. Orange hair."

"That color hair is called red, not orange," Eric said. "And it's a wig."

"You were right," Cam told Eric when she got back to the bush. "The man in the bookstore had hair. Here it is. The man inside the house probably wore this so people wouldn't know who he was. He's the one who took Poochie."

"What are we going to do now?" Diane asked.

Eric turned to answer Diane. "We should call the police."

Then Eric turned to tell Cam that he was going back. But she wasn't there. She was near the house, looking through an open window.

Donna and Diane ran over to Cam and looked through the window. Eric stayed near the bush. He was still holding Cloudy.

"He's in there," Cam said. "I can see him in the next room. He's sitting at a desk and cutting things out of a magazine."

Cam and the twins watched the man turn

the pages of a magazine. Sometimes he would stop, cut out something and paste it onto a sheet of paper. Then he folded the paper and put it into a green envelope.

"I wonder what's in that envelope," Cam said.

"Look," Donna said. "He's getting up. And there's Poochie under the desk."

Suddenly Cloudy barked and jumped out of Eric's arms. Cam caught him before he could run away.

"Cloudy wants to go into the house," Eric said.

Cam looked at Cloudy. Then she looked at the window and said, "That gives me an idea."

Cam asked the twins to stand next to each other. "Now undo your braids," Cam told Donna.

Donna took the rubber bands off the ends of her braids. Then she ran her fingers through her hair.

40

Cam looked closely at the two girls. Each one was wearing blue shorts, a polka dot blouse, and sneakers. "Without the braids," Cam said, "you two look exactly alike."

"That's why I wear braids sometimes," Donna said. "I don't like it when people call me Diane."

"And I don't like being called by your name," Diane said.

"You can braid your hair again in just a few minutes," Cam said. "But right now are you willing to help get Poochie back?"

The two girls said, "Yes."

"Good. Now here's the plan."

Chapter Seven

It wasn't easy for Cam to talk. She was holding Cloudy, and the dog wouldn't stop licking Cam's face.

Cam wiped her cheek. Then she said, "We have to get the man away from his desk. If we do that, we can switch the dogs."

Cloudy licked Cam's face again. Cam wiped her cheek and went on with her plan.

"If Donna taps on one of the closed windows, the man will run over to see who's there. Before he can open the window, Diane can tap on another window. The man will run to the other window. If you two take turns tapping on windows, the man will be busy running from one window to the other. And while he's running, I'll switch the dogs."

"It's a good plan," Diane said.

"The best part of the plan," Eric said, "is that since you two look so much alike, he'll think he's seeing the same girl at both windows. He'll wonder how anyone can run so fast from one window to the other."

Eric told Cam that he would let her know if the man was going back to his desk.

Donna walked up to one of the windows at the side of the house. Diane went to another window near the front door. Eric hid behind a bush and watched them both.

Cam walked back to the open window. She saw the man sitting at his desk. He was holding the green envelope.

When Cloudy saw the man, he tried to jump out of Cam's arms. But Cam held on to him.

"Just stop it. You'll be in there soon," Cam told the dog.

But Cloudy would not stop. And when he could not get out of Cam's arms, he barked.

"Is that you, Cloudy?" the man called out. He started to walk toward the open window.

"Oh, no," Cam said as she moved away from the window. "You've ruined everything, Cloudy."

Tap. Tap.

Donna was tapping at one of the closed windows.

"Oh," Cam whispered to Cloudy, "I hope he goes to see who it is."

He did. Cam heard the man call through the closed window, "What do you want?"

Tap. Tap.

It was Diane tapping at another window.
Cam heard the man run to the other
window.

This is my chance, Cam thought. She let
Cloudy jump through the open window.

Then she called, "Here, Poochie. Here, Poochie."

Poochie started to walk toward the window. Then he saw Cloudy.

"*Woof.*"

"*Woof. Woof.*"

"Here, Poochie. Here, Poochie," Cam called again.

Poochie walked past Cloudy. He was almost at the window when he turned around.

"Stop that tapping," the man yelled.

Eric called to Cam, "You better hurry and get Poochie."

"Come here. Come back, Poochie," Cam called. But Poochie didn't listen. He walked toward the desk and Cloudy.

"Stop it already!" the man yelled again.

Tap. Tap.

"That's it. I'm going outside."

"Quick, girls, hide here with me," Eric called out.

The twins ran to Eric. Then the front door opened. The man looked around, but he didn't see either of the twins.

"Here, Poochie," Cam called again.

Poochie jumped onto the desk, grabbed the green envelope in his mouth, and then jumped off. Poochie walked slowly toward

the window. He looked ahead as he walked and his tail pointed up.

"Stay away from my house!" the man at

the front door yelled. Then he went inside and slammed the front door shut.

Oh, no, Cam thought. *If he sees both dogs together, we'll never get Poochie back.*

Chapter Eight

Before the man returned to his desk, Poochie jumped onto the windowsill. Then he jumped into Cam's arms.

Cam took the green envelope out of Poochie's mouth. She was ready to open it when she saw the man sit at his desk and then reach down to pet Cloudy.

Cam put the envelope in her pocket and waited. Would the man notice that the dogs had been switched?

"Good dog. Good Poochie," the man said as he petted Cloudy.

Eric and the twins ran up to Cam. Eric was carrying the shopping bag.

"Which dog are you holding?" Eric asked Cam.

"Poochie."

"You switched them?"

"Yes," Cam said. "And he doesn't even know we have Poochie. Let's get back to the bookstore before he finds out."

"We did it!" Donna said.

Cam held Poochie as they all squeezed through the same hole in the fence they had gone through earlier. Then Cam put Poochie down and they walked to Lee's Bookstore.

"We have Poochie," Donna told Mr. Lee as they walked into the bookstore.

Two policemen were standing there with Mr. Lee and Poochie's trainer. "Is that the missing dog?" one of the policemen asked.

The trainer looked at Poochie and said, "I think so. But I'm not sure."

"This *is* Poochie," Donna said. "Just watch."

Donna picked up Poochie and put him on the table. "Now raise your right paw," she told the dog.

Poochie raised his right paw.

"Now show us what a sad dog looks like."

Poochie looked down at the table. His tail stopped wagging.

"Well, if this is Poochie, where's the man who took him?" Mr. Lee asked.

"I can tell you that," Cam said, and she closed her eyes and said, *"Click."*

"His address was painted on the post near his front door. It's 625 Dogwood Lane."

Cam, Eric, and the twins waited in the bookstore while the police went to pick up the man. When the police came back, the bald man was with them.

"I did take Poochie," the man said, "but it was a mistake. I thought he was Cloudy."

Poochie barked. Then he walked across the table to Cam. With his mouth, Poochie took the green envelope out of Cam's pocket and took it to one of the policemen.

The policeman opened the envelope. He took out a sheet of paper.

"Well, look at this. It's a note written with letters cut from a magazine. You didn't want us to be able to trace your handwrit-

ing. And this note says that you will give
Poochie back only after a ransom is paid.

"When you took Poochie, it was not a
mistake."

"And this isn't a mistake either," the
other policeman said. "You're coming with
us."

Chapter Nine

After the policemen left the bookstore with the man, Mr. Lee told Poochie's trainer, "These children should get a reward."

"Yes, they should," the trainer said. He reached into his pocket and took out a small card.

"What are your names?" he asked Cam.

"Eric Shelton, Donna Shelton, Diane Shelton, and I'm Jennifer Jansen."

The trainer wrote the names on the card. Then Poochie pressed his paw onto the ink pad and then onto the card.

"This is a pass for all of you to come to our studio and watch a Poochie television program being filmed."

"Could we have a pass for Howie—he's our baby brother—and for our parents?" Donna asked.

"Of course," the trainer said, and he added the names to the pass. "I'll also have four Poochie battery-operated toy dogs and four Poochie memory games sent here. If you come back in a few days, you can pick them up from Mr. Lee."

"Oh, good," Cam said. "I love memory games."

Then Eric took *The Poochie Story* out of the shopping bag. "And could the *real* Poochie sign our book?" he asked.

Poochie signed the book. Then Cam, Eric, and the twins shook hands with Mr. Lee, the trainer, and Poochie.

At the door Donna and Diane waved to Poochie.

"*Woof. Woof,*" Poochie barked, and wagged his tail.

As they walked away from the bookstore,

Cam held up her hands and said, "My hands have ink on them."

"So do mine," said Eric, Donna, and Diane, all at the same time.

Cam smiled and said, "Well, then that really was the *real* Poochie."